CRABBY GABBY

Written by Stephen Cosgrove
Illustrated by Robin James

A Serendipity™ Book

PRICE STERN SLOAN

Dedicated to Roby LaPorte and Carolyn Davis. Often Gabby, rarely crabby, and always the best of friends.

– Stephen

Far beyond the horizon, in the middle of the Crystal Sea is a magical island that is known as Serendipity.

Inland from the shore is a land filled with velvet trees and giggling, wandering streams. It is a place where all wishes come true and nothing happens that you don't want to.

It was in this place that certain fuzzy, big-eyed creatures called Furry Eyefulls lived. Their lives were nothing more than a search for beautiful things to see. They would wander from valley to valley, looking at a little bit of this and a little bit of that.

One special Furry Eyefull, bigger of eye than the rest and a little more talkative than most, was Gabby. She not only wanted to see all that she could see, but had to tell everyone about it as they were seeing it, too.

Day in and day out Gabby was the one who suggested what the Furry Eyefulls did for the day. She awakened everyone in the morning with her excited chatter about all the things they would do and see.

"Wake up! Wake up! It's time for a new Gabby-Game!" she shouted eagerly. "Today we must see where the river pours into the sea!" One by one, the Furries woke with a stretch and a yawn and followed Gabby to another beautiful sight.

Day by day, week by week, Gabby suggested this and suggested that in all her Gabby-Games. But soon the suggestions turned into requests and the requests turned into demands.

"Come on! Come on! I have a new Gabby-Game!" she shouted. "We must go see the parading peacocks!"

The whole gaggle of Furry Eyefulls rushed to see the peacocks. They settled into the gentle meadow moss and prepared to watch for hours and hours. Then, just as the peacocks fanned their gorgeous tails, Gabby rushed them off to another sight.

"Hurry! Hurry! We must get to Mirror Lake to watch the silver fish flash in the noontime sun!" she demanded. As always the Furry Eyefulls followed, waddling down the path that wound through the forest.

After they had sat by the lake for a time or two, Gabby jumped to her fuzzy feet and said, dusting the leaves from her fur, "Well, that's enough of that. Now we are all going deep into the forest to throw nuts and pinecones at the chipmunks. It's one of my most favorite Gabby-Games. Come on, guys let's go!" And with that, they all stood and started to leave.

But one of the younger Furry Eyefulls spoke up, "Uh, I really don't want to play another Gabby-Game. Why don't we all just sit here and continue to watch the fish in the lake?"

Well, Gabby was fit to be tied. "Why don't you just sit there, then?" she asked sarcastically. "In fact why don't you play the new Gabby-Game with your friends, the fish?" Then she pushed him into the lake. The other Furry Eyefulls laughed and laughed as the younger one tried to climb from the water with a lily-pad on his head. Then, happily they followed Gabby up the trail.

The Eyefulls waddled to the middle of the forest to the tall stately hazelnut tree in which all the chipmunks lived. Gabby picked up a pinecone and threw it, narrowly missing a tiny chipmunk that scampered out of the way. All the Furries began throwing hazelnuts and pinecones at the other chipmunks that stood chattering angrily in the branches.

Gabby just laughed and laughed to see the chipmunks ducking this way and that. Copying Gabby, all the other Furry Eyefulls joined in her giggling and laughter.

It seemed like such a good Gabby-Game.

Finally one of the Furries said, "Hey, maybe we shouldn't be doing this. After all, the poor little chipmunks have a right to be in the forest, too!"

Gabby looked at her in disbelief. "Oh, you like the little chipmunks, huh? Well, if you like the chipmunks so much you can have all of their hazelnuts!" And with that, she threw a handful of nuts in her face and ran off down the path.

The others did the same, and then chased after Gabby leaving the crying Furry Eyefull all alone.

Later that very same day Gabby led everyone into the meadow to play a game with her ball. "Hurry! Hurry!" she yelled. "We're going to play a brand-new Gabby-Game."

"What is a Gabby-Game?" someone asked.

Gabby quickly answered, "Silly, a Gabby-Game is a game where Gabby makes up all the rules and everybody has to play."

"Well, that doesn't seem very fair," another little Furry said.

"Well," said Gabby, "you don't have to play, but it is my ball. So, it's a Gabby Game or nothing."

All but one Furry Eyefull decided to play, looking to Gabby for the rules of the brand-new Gabby-Game.

So she explained the rules of her Gabby-Game. "First everyone throws the ball to me and then I throw the ball to someone else. The winner is the one who catches the ball the most."

"Wait a minute," said one of the Eyefulls. "If we always have to throw the ball back to you then you will always win!"

"Of course!" she laughed. "After all, it's my ball and this is a Gabby-Game!"

All the other Eyefulls looked at one another and then back at Gabby, who was juggling the ball from one hand to the other.

"You know," said the Eyefulls, "We have gone from pond to stream to see and do only those things that you wanted to see and do. We don't want to play your Gabby-Games anymore!"

Then they all walked away, leaving Gabby alone in the meadow with her favorite ball and her only friend . . . herself.

"Pooh! What do they know? They'll find that without me there isn't any fun, just wait and see." With the ball as a pillow, she stretched out in the cool grasses of the meadow, waiting for them to return.

She waited and waited and finally fell asleep dreaming selfish dreams of always winning her Gabby-Games.

When she woke she found that she was still alone. The other Furry Eyefulls had not come back. "Silly fur balls!" she muttered. "Well, I had better show them who's the boss!" Gabby set off in search of her friends through the forest of ferns. She searched and searched and finally found the group of them sitting in a tiny meadow staring at a bed of blooming flowers.

"Hey, it's time for a new Gabby-Game!" she announced cheerfully. "Come on, everybody who wants to play, follow me! We're going to throw nuts at the chipmunks again! Come on! Follow me!"

She raced back through the forest to the old hazel nut tree where the chipmunks lived. Excited, she turned around only to discover that she was alone.

With a thump she sat on an old rotted stump and began to cry. It seemed nobody wanted to play her Gabby-Games anymore.

As she cried, a kindly, blind snake called Kartusch coiled himself on a rock behind her in the meadow. "Why do you cry, little one?" hissed the snake softly.

"None of the other Furry Eyefulls want to play my Gabby-Games anymore."

Kartusch thought for a moment. "Gabby," he said, "the other Furry Eyefulls don't want to play anymore because you don't know how to share. You only want to be the leader, but the best of leaders are those who have learned to share the lead and follow. When you are ready to share you will always win even though you may lose the game."

Gabby's tears slowly dried in the warmth of Kartusch's words, and she knew that he was right.

Day after day Gabby learned to share with the other Furry Eyefulls. She played a new Gabby-Game called share the leader, where she let the others make up games and she even shared her ball even though she rarely won.

WHEN THE BALL IS YOURS

AND YOU START TO PLAY

A SELFISH GABBY-GAME,

INSTEAD PLAY SHARE THE LEADER

LET IT BE SOMEONE ELSE'S GAME.

Serendipity™ *Books*

Created by
Stephen Cosgrove and Robin James

Enjoy all the delightful books in the Serendipity™ *Series:*

Available wherever books are sold.

PRICE STERN SLOAN